GRADUATION DAY

Adapted by Tracey West

SCHOLASTIC INC.

The publisher does not have any control over and does not assume any responsibility for author or third-party websites or their content.

This book is a work of fiction. Names, characters, places, and incidents are either the product of the author's imagination or are used fictitiously, and any resemblance to actual persons, living or dead, business establishments, events, or locales is entirely coincidental.

ISBN 978-1-338-11478-2

12 11 10 9 8 7 6 5 4 3 2 1   16 17 18 19 20 21

Printed in the U.S.A.   40

This edition first printing, September 2016

Book design by Rick DeMonico

CHAPTER 1

The entire kingdom is abuzz with excitement, Alice!" said joust announcer Herb Herbertson.

"I'm certainly excited, Herb!" agreed his partner, Alice Squires. "And abuzz!"

Herb looked like an average announcer, while Alice was a Squirebot. But they were a lot alike. Both announcers had perfect hair, big smiles, and even bigger voices.

They sat in a booth inside the Joustdome, a gleaming metal and glass dome-shaped arena in the city of Knightonia, the capital of the kingdom of Knighton. Below them, citizens and Squirebots took their seats. Other

Squirebots roamed the aisles, selling snacks and knight souvenirs.

A cheer rose from the crowd as King and Queen Halbert stepped into their royal balcony. The king's bushy ginger beard could be seen from the farthest seat.

"The king and queen have arrived, so the festivities can officially begin!" Herb announced.

"And they look so radiant for the 151st Annual Knights' Academy Graduation Ceremony!" added Alice.

Herb nodded. "There's a small class of five knights graduating today," he said. "Not much for a knight to do since it's been peaceful here in the realm for more than a hundred years."

"It's going to be an amazing show featuring Merlok the Magician and Jestro the Royal Jester!" Alice promised. "Now, the big question on everyone's minds: Will Princess Macy

Halbert be allowed to become a Knight of the Realm with her classmates?"

"Well, she did graduate second in her class, Alice," Herb reminded her.

Over in the royal balcony, a young woman with dark red hair and freckles was talking to the king and queen. She wore a suit of armor with a red dragon sigil on the chest.

"Dad, you promised I could graduate!" Macy said.

"Princess, you know I don't want you going out and doing any of that messy fighting," King Halbert said.

"I want to be a knight, Dad. It's what I was meant to be." She turned to the queen. "Mom? Talk to him!"

Queen Halbert looked at her husband. "You did promise, dear," she reminded him. "And we haven't had any fighting in our kingdom for a hundred years."

"Oh, all right," King Halbert relented.

"Yes!" Macy cried, rushing off to join the others.

"But no fighting, young lady!" her father called after her.

It was time for the ceremony to begin.

"Let's introduce you to the stars of this show—the newest knights of the realm! Ready for their Graduation Battle-bration!" Herb announced.

Flashing lights shot out of the arena's stage entrance and a rugged knight walked out. He wore silver armor and a dark blue helmet. On his chest was the symbol of a blue-and-white eagle against a dark blue background. He twirled his sword in front of him.

"It's the knights' knight, Clay Moorington!" said Alice. "I don't think anyone expected this country boy to be at the top of his class."

Next emerged a grinning blond knight. His armor bore the symbol of a white horse against a light blue background. He held up a weapon that looked like a long, sharp pole attached to a high-tech handle.

"It's lucky Lance Richmond and his amazingly lithe lance!" declared Alice.

"Boy, I wish I could be him," said Herb.

"Doesn't everyone?" asked Alice.

The third knight flew into the arena on a hoverboard. He had bright red hair, and his armor was accented with green. He held a crossbow and played it like a guitar. His symbol was an orange fox against a green background.

"The thrill-seeker, Aaron Fox!" said Herb.

"He's got 'mad skillz,' as the kids say," added Alice.

The fourth knight stomped into the arena. He was twice as big as the others, and he wore a gold helmet with metal horns sticking out of each side. His symbol was a golden bull against a purple background, and he carried a giant, double-bladed axe.

"It's big, bad Axl!" shouted Herb.

"And his big, bad axe!" finished Alice.

After Axl, Macy jumped into the arena, holding a weapon that looked like a big, glowing hammer.

"And the amazing Macy joins in!" cried Herb.

"I never doubted it for a second," said Alice.

"Except when you did just a minute ago," Herb reminded her softly. Then he switched to his big announcer voice. "And we'll be back to start the official Graduation Battle-bration in a few minutes, folks! Stay tuned!"

Backstage at the arena, a crew worked busily to make sure the celebration would go smoothly. In a few minutes, the knights would begin to demonstrate their skills.

Handling the tech were two students at the Knights' Academy, Ava Prentis and Robin Underwood. Ava had brown hair and eyes that always looked like they were searching for answers. Robin had wavy, sandy blond hair and wore an armor plate over his light blue uniform. His symbol was a cute white chicken on a blue background.

"I wish I could be out there graduating and becoming a knight," grumbled Robin.

"We're only freshmen at the academy, Robin," Ava reminded him. "We're just lucky they let us coordinate these dummies."

She pointed to two grinning Squirebots. Each one had a spinning target attached to a short pole on top of his helmet.

"Uh, I meant *target* dummies," Ava corrected herself.

"Hey, we volunteered for this," said the first squire cheerfully.

"Yeah, we like being dummies!" said the second, just as cheerfully.

"Okay, let's give them a good show, everybody!" Robin called out.

"It'll be, um, interesting, I'll guarantee that," said Ava.

Meanwhile, Clay was looking for the other knights. He found Lance reclining on a massage chair in the training room. One Squirebot was trimming his fingernails, and another was polishing his armor.

"Lance, I've prepared a rundown for each of us on the specific battle moves we should highlight in our Graduation Battle-bration," Clay told him.

He handed Lance a tablet with a digital graphic of the plan. Lance handed it to one of the Squirebots, who tossed it over his shoulder.

"Relax, would you, Super Knight?" Lance asked. "We're going to graduate no matter what."

"It's important that we make a good impression," Clay reminded him.

Lance grinned. "I do that just by being me."

Clay sighed. "Have you seen Merlok? I need to talk to him."

"Who knows what that old wizard is up to," Lance replied. "I'll give you all the advice you need: Just spin your sword around, smile, and they'll all love you. Not as much as they love me, but we all knew that."

Clay rolled his eyes and walked away. Nearby, Macy, Axl, and Aaron were getting ready for the performance.

"You nervous, Axl?" Macy asked.

"Nope," he answered in his deep voice. "I'm hungry."

"You're always hungry," quipped Aaron.

Clay walked in. "But you're about to become an official knight!" he said. "Have you thought about how important that is?"

"Hmmm," Axl mused. "Will it get me an extra slice of cake?"

Music blared through the arena.

"That's our cue," said Aaron, picking up his crossbow and plucking the string like it was a guitar. "Time for a bow-dacious Battle-bration!"

The crowd clapped and cheered as the Squirebots marched out into the arena. Some of them held wooden targets, while others had targets attached to their helmets.

Clay strode into the arena with a determined look on his face.

"The sensational super-swordplay of Clay Moorington!" Herb announced.

Clay spun his sword around in preparation and then charged the first Squirebot.

Swoosh! With one swipe of his blade, he sliced through the digital target on top of the nervous bot's head. The target fizzled out.

Swoosh! Swoosh! Swoosh! Clay jumped from one Squirebot to the next, slicing each target as the crowd hollered its approval.

"Merlok the Magician really helped Clay be all the knight he could be," said Alice.

"Yup, Merlok's friendship and advice sure paid off," agreed Herb. "Oh look, it's Aaron Fox!"

Aaron zipped into the arena riding his hoverboard. Three Squirebots raced past him, each one balancing a red apple on his helmet.

"Woo-hoo!" cheered Aaron. He aimed his crossbow at the Squirebots and shot an arrow toward them.

Whoosh! The arrow sliced through the first apple, then the second, then the third . . . perfect!

"Aaron Fox, the airborne archer! He's simply off the hook!" said Alice.

Aaron landed next to Clay and fist-bumped him. Then Lance came out, riding his gleaming mecha horse.

"Lance Richmond is always so polished," remarked Herb.

"He's the shiniest knight I've ever seen!" Alice cried, her blue bot eyes gleaming.

Lance lowered his weapon and charged at a Squirebot who was also riding a mecha horse. This was a classic joust. The two would ride at each other head-on, and each had to try to knock off the other using his lance.

The Squirebot charged at Lance with

amazing speed. Startled, Lance sped right past him without trying to knock him down.

"Ha ha! You missed!" the bot taunted.

Lance had failed! But that couldn't happen. Not to Lance.

How am I going to fix this? Lance wondered.

Lance turned his head to look at the Squirebot—and his hover horse crashed into the barrier! Acting on instinct, Lance lowered his lance. It bent like a spring, sending him flying across the arena.

Lance tumbled through the air—and then regained his balance. With a cry, he leapt onto the Squirebot's mecha horse, knocking the bot right out of his seat. Lance took control of the horse and flew triumphantly around the arena as the crowd cheered.

"I planned that," he said as he pulled up to Clay.

"Yeah, sure," Clay replied.

14

Then big Axl stomped into the arena.

"And here comes Axl! He's always hungry for action," Alice remarked.

"I don't want to get between him and the dinner buffet!" Herb joked.

Axl stared at a giant punching bag full of Squirebots. He was supposed to attack the punching bag with his axe. But that would take too long, and Axl was hungry! Instead, he slammed his axe into the ground.

Boom! The axe's vibrations caused the bag to open and the Squirebots spilled out, crashing into the dirt.

Satisfied, Axl walked over to the others, munching a sandwich.

"Axl the Ever-Hungry gives way to Princess Macy Halbert," announced Herb.

Macy ran out into the arena. Her helmet had metal bars caging in her determined face. She was about to show everyone that she was born to be a knight.

A Squirebot operating a giant mecha-bot stomped toward her. Macy grunted and charged toward him.

She jumped in the air, landed on the mecha-bot's shoulder, and kicked. As she flew off the robot, it fell forward, right on its face.

The mecha-bot got back on its feet, and Macy activated her power mace. It glowed with power as she leapt forward.

"Ha!" Macy cried, swinging the mace.

Bam! She knocked the mecha-robot's head right off! The crowd cheered as she landed firmly on two feet.

"Wow! That's a-*mace*-ing!" cried Alice, and Herb grimaced at the terrible pun.

She joined the other four knights on a platform and it rose up to the royal balcony. The king and queen clapped for them.

"Good citizens of this land!" began King Halbert in a booming voice. "We welcome these new knights of the realm and present them with the symbols of their achievement—

the Knightronic Shields of the kingdom, bearing their family crests."

Squirebots came out with four shields bearing symbols that matched the markings on the knights' armor. But there were only four Squirebots and four shields—and none bore the symbol of a dragon.

"Where's my shield, Dad?" Macy asked her father.

"We'll discuss this later," King Halbert said.

Macy gritted her teeth. "This is so unfair."

Axl, Clay, and Lance powered up their shields and turned to the crowd. Aaron jumped on his and hovered above the others.

"Whoa! This makes an awesome hover shield," he said.

Clay frowned. "You know what that is? It's disrespectful. With a capital *D*."

Lance bopped Clay on the head with his lance. "Lighten up, uber-knight. This is supposed to be a party."

King Halbert turned back to the arena. "Ladies and gentlemen, the Knights' Academy graduates of . . ."

"ROOOOAAAAAR!"

Smoke poured into the arena. Fire exploded from the entrance. A huge monster emerged from the flames, growling and charging the royal booth. His huge body looked like it was sculpted from molten rock. Lava seemed to flow through his veins. His eyes glowed with yellow fire inside his massive skull, and sharp teeth jutted from his jaw.

Two more glowing monsters emerged behind him!

"Monsters? There haven't been monsters here in a hundred years!" cried Alice.

Herb jumped into her arms. "I'm so scared!"

Queen Halbert grabbed a shield from off the wall and tossed it to her daughter.

"Macy! Use this!" she cried.

The five knights put on their helmets.

"Knights! Defend the people of the realm!" Clay cried, raising his sword.

The platform lowered and the five knights charged into the arena. Clay swung his sword at the leg of one of the monsters—but as he did, the monster flickered and disappeared.

"Huh?" wondered Clay as the monster reappeared, unharmed, in front of him.

Axl swung his battle-axe at a monster, but the big beast dodged the blows. Aaron shot his crossbow at a monster. The arrows glowed brightly when they made contact, but then fizzled out.

Macy jumped up and swung her mace at a monster with all her might. The mace went right through it and she landed on the ground with a thud.

"We've got to coordinate our attacks!" Clay yelled. "Lance, drive your monster toward me!"

"Like you know better," Lance scoffed. "I can handle this thing."

He ran toward the nearest monster and threw his lance. It passed right through the monster and hit Axl in the chest. He toppled back, knocking down Macy. Then the lance hit Aaron, knocking him out of the sky. He smashed right into Clay!

The three monsters surrounded the fallen knights. Things looked grim . . . until, suddenly, they all vanished!

A tornado of golden light swirled into the arena. The light faded to reveal a wizard in blue robes with a long, white beard.

"Ha! That was a good trick, wasn't it?"

CHAPTER 4

T is I, Merlok the Magician!" the wizard announced. He raised his magic staff in the air and sparks shot out of it. "This is supposed to be a celebration!"

Macy turned to Clay and smiled. "It was Merlok. That's a relief."

"Good show, Merlok," said King Halbert. "You truly are the greatest wizard in the realm."

A sad look crossed Merlok's face. "I'm also the only wizard left in the realm."

Then he looked up at the knights and smiled. "Our new knights: While you may be graduating, you must recognize that you still have much to learn. And now, for a little magic."

He swung his staff and pointed it at the knights. Sparkling, golden light poured out.

"*Horus Porus Disappearum!*" the wizard yelled.

The knights vanished into the golden light, and then fireworks exploded over the arena. Merlok bowed to the cheers of the crowd.

Then golden light sparkled again, and the five knights reappeared on the platform. It raised up again as the crowd went wild.

The knights and Merlok went backstage, where Jestro, the court jester, was waiting to perform. He wore a purple-and-blue costume and his face was painted clown white. The bells around his neck jangled as he paced back and forth.

Clay walked up to him. "Hey, Jestro. You're up next," he said. "Don't worry so much. You'll be great."

"I'm kind of nervous, Clay," Jestro admitted. "Never follow a better act, they say, and the people all love Merlok."

"Love is a strong word," Lance chimed in. "I'd say, 'adore,' or maybe 'cherish.'"

"Look, if anyone laughs at you I'll give them a haircut with my sword," Clay promised kindly.

"I'm the jester—they're supposed to laugh at me," Jestro said.

"Uh, yeah, that's what I meant," said Clay. "Just stay positive. You'll be fine."

Jestro nodded. "Right. Time for some comedy!"

"That's the spirit!" Clay encouraged as Jestro walked away.

"Is he going to crash and burn?" Lance whispered.

"No, no. Of course not," Clay said.

"But probably," Lance said.

Clay sighed. "Yeah." He had been Jestro's friend for years. Jestro was a good guy, but a terrible jester.

Jestro knew it, too. But being the court jester was an important job, and he always tried to do his best.

As he stepped out onto the arena floor, he decided to go for a spectacular entrance. He did a handstand and then tried to backflip—and fell right onto his face. The crowd laughed and clapped, thinking it was part of the act.

"You can do this," Jestro told himself as he picked himself up. "Be funny."

He raised his arms. "Hey, it's good to be here!" he yelled to the crowd. "But I'm always here. I live here!"

Some of the crowd laughed—but the rest groaned. Jestro knew he had to step it up.

He moved on to his spinning plate trick, where he kept six spinning plates balanced on top of six spikes. A good plate spinner could keep it up for a long time—but Jestro's plates crashed after only a few seconds of spinning.

Next, he tried his tablecloth trick. In the center of the arena was a table topped with a tablecloth and all the ingredients of a royal feast. To impress the crowd, all he had to do was remove the tablecloth without disturbing any of the food.

Jestro yanked the tablecloth—and the food went flying! Apples, carrots, and a pumpkin pie bonked him on the head. Then a roast turkey slipped right over his head! He stumbled around with a turkey on his head, and the crowd booed him.

King Halbert was fond of Jestro and wanted him to do well.

"Do the juggling!" he called out. "Everyone loves juggling!"

Jestro grabbed a sword, a mace, and a spear and began to juggle them, humming as he tossed the weapons above his head. Backstage, the knights and Merlok watched the action on a big screen.

"Does he know that's a power mace?" Macy asked.

"Does that make a difference?" Lance wondered.

"It might," Macy replied.

Clay was worried for his friend. "You can do it, Jestro," he said under his breath.

The unimpressed crowd started to boo, so Jestro tried to juggle faster and faster. Sweat broke out on his forehead. He gripped the mace as it came back down, and the weapon powered on.

"*Aaaaaaaaaaah!*" Jestro cried as the charge shocked him. He let go of the mace, and it flew across the arena. The crowd gasped and ducked as the electrically-charged mace flew over their heads.

Then . . . *bam!* It hit the power grid on the arena wall.

The area lights flickered, then turned off. Soon the power outage surged throughout the city. All of Knightonia was in darkness!

CHAPTER 5

Wow, Alice! Jestro finishes his act with a power outage!" Herb announced, looking around the darkened arena.

"I've heard of bringing the house down, but bringing the power down?" Alice asked, laughing. "Get it?"

"Yeah, I get it," Herb said, shaking his head.

Back on the arena floor, Jestro ran toward the entrance—and banged right into Clay.

"Oh, I'm a horrible failure!" Jestro moaned. "I can't do anything right!"

"Come on, nobody thinks that," Clay assured him.

"You're a horrible failure!" yelled a Squirebot from the stands.

"You can't do anything right!" chimed in another Squirebot.

Jestro burst into tears and ran off.

"Jestro, wait! I want to talk to you!" Clay called after him.

King Halbert knew he had to calm down the frightened crowd. "All is well! Even though darkness falls across the land!"

His words had the opposite effect. The crowd started to panic.

"Uh, I didn't mean it like that," he said. "It is dark, but not evil, world-ending, soul-sucking darkness."

That did it. Everyone began to scream and run.

"You're not helping, dear," said the queen gently.

Jestro had already fled to the dark castle. He walked down the deserted halls, feel-ing miserable.

"Another big chance, and I blew it!" he scolded himself. "I'm just bad at everything!"

Then a voice came out of nowhere.

"I bet you could be good at being bad, jester!"

Jestro gasped. "Are you talking to me?"

"See any other jesters around?" the voice asked. "No, you're not hearing things. And you're not talking to yourself, either. Come find me. I'm in Merlok's library."

Curious, Jestro walked to the wizard's library and pushed open the big doors. He cautiously stepped inside.

"This place is usually locked up," he said out loud.

"Yeah, your little power outage trick unlocked the door," the voice explained.

Jestro walked toward the sound of the voice. It was close. Was it coming from that chair?

He jumped in front of the chair. "Aha!" he cried. But nobody was sitting in it.

"No, no, no," the voice said. "Over here."

Jestro looked around and spotted a large, open book on a stand all by itself. Golden light sparkled around it.

Jestro reached through the light, and it flickered out. He picked up the book and closed it.

"Boo!"

"Aaah!" shrieked Jestro.

There was a face on the cover of the book! Not a picture, but a living face. Two yellow eyes with red pupils glowed above a wide mouth filled with sharp teeth.

"Ha! I love doing that," the book said. "You shoulda seen your face."

"You're a book?" Jestro asked. He still couldn't believe what he was seeing.

"I'm THE book—The Book of Monsters," the book replied. "And I think I could make you the baddest baddie in the realm."

Jestro shook his head. "I don't know . . ."

"You want to have everybody laugh at you? You want to be a joke?" the book asked. "How many more times do you want to be the laughingstock of the whole kingdom?"

The book's words hit home for Jestro. He thought about all of the people and Squirebots in the stands, laughing at him. His eyes filled with tears again.

"Ah, quit living in the past!" the book said, and then chomped on Jestro's hands.

"Hey, you bit me!" Jestro cried.

"I had to snap you out of sad-face clown-boy mode," said The Book of Monsters. "I can make you somebody! A guy who's respected. I can make you the most feared guy in the whole land. That's gotta be better than spinning plates, right?"

Jestro slowly nodded. "Okay. I'm listening."

"Look around: There's lots of power in these books," the book said. "I know them all. Grab as many as you can and let's jail-break this musty old place."

Jestro looked around at the shelves and shelves of books. Did they really hold the power the book said they did? And could he really change his life? Stop being the jester who everyone laughed at?

Maybe. Just maybe.

He started to frantically grab books from the shelf.

"That's it, kid, grab them all," The Book of Monsters instructed. "And you'll need a magic staff to make my pages come to life. Merlok has a dozen of them lying around."

Jestro spotted a staff with a spiked circle on the top. He grabbed it just as Clay walked into the library.

"Jestro? You in here?" Clay called into the dark library. "I wanted to talk to you."

"It's that goody-goody knight!" fumed the book. "Quick, page 205! Wave the magic staff over me and conjure a monster."

"But it's Clay," Jestro said. "He's, like, my friend."

"Nobody's your friend but me, joke-boy! Remember that! Now quick, page 205!"

Jestro quickly paged through The Book of Monsters. When he found page 205, he saw that it was filled with pictures of monsters. They were all moving, struggling to get out of the book.

Clay spotted him. "Jestro, what are you doing?"

"Do it!" The Book of Monsters hissed.

Jestro pointed the staff at the page. He jumped back as a glowing red arm thrust out of the book. Then another arm. Then a huge, monster body with spiked shoulders, horns, and one enormous eye in its head.

"*Roooooaaaaar!*" bellowed the monster.

"It's Sparkks!" cried The Book of Monsters.

Jestro looked up at the huge creature. Like the monster in Merlok's trick, its body looked like it was sculpted from molten rock. Lava flowed through its veins. But this was no trick.

This was real.

"What have I done?" Jestro cried.

CHAPTER 6

The Book of Monsters laughed. "This is gonna be one monstrous take-down," he said gleefully. "See, kid? You're good at something. You're good at being bad!"

Sparkks growled, and Clay charged toward him with his sword raised. He jumped in the air and swung the sword down hard toward the monster.

Clunk! It bounced harmlessly off the monster's rock-hard head.

Then Sparkks kicked Clay. The knight flew across the room and slammed into a bookshelf.

Clay tumbled to the floor, picked himself up, and grabbed his sword.

"*Rooaaaaar!*" Sparkks charged him again.

Clay thought quickly. He looked up and saw the heavy wooden chandelier hanging from the ceiling. He jumped onto a hover disc used to reach the tall library shelves. He rode it until he reached the chandelier. The huge fixture was as big as the monster.

"*Aaaargh!*" With all his might, Clay swung his sword at the metal pole connecting the chandelier to the ceiling. He jumped to the floor as the heavy, wooden fixture landed right on Sparkks's head.

Sparkks was floored. But he got back up again, growling, and smashed the chandelier into toothpicks.

"More monsters! Make more monsters!" The Book of Monsters cried.

Jestro waved his wand over the book again. From the book sprung Globlins—bouncing fireballs. Then came Bloblins—bigger, bouncing fireballs. Finally came Scurriers—little red creatures with arms and legs that looked like they were made of pure flame.

Giggling with evil glee, the Globlins and Bloblins bounced at Clay. He batted them aside with his sword. Then came the Scurriers. He swiped at them, too, but there were just too many.

Sensing a moment of weakness, Sparkks swung at Clay with a mighty fist.

Bam! The blow sent the knight flying across the room and crashing to the floor. This time, he couldn't get up.

The library doors swung open, and Merlok stepped inside.

"That crazy ol' Merlok. I hate him!" complained The Book of Monsters. "Now here's our chance—destroy them both!"

The smaller Magma Monsters advanced toward Merlok and the fallen Clay.

"Jestro, stop this!" Merlok cried, pointing his staff at the jester.

He raised the staff over his head and twirled it like a baton. The globe at the end of the staff began to glow with yellow light.

"You . . . shall not . . . be monstrous!" Merlok cried with great effort, and then slammed the end of the staff onto the floor.

Whoosh! A wave of golden light swept all of the monsters back, even Sparkks. But as soon as the light faded, the monsters charged forward again.

Merlok slowly backed up. Behind him, Clay rose to his feet.

The wizard pointed a hand at Clay. A beam of golden light shot out, zapping him. Clay went flying out of the library doors, and then they slammed shut, locking him out.

"Yes! Finish him!" The Book of Monsters cried.

The monsters ran at Merlok. He began to twirl his staff again, this time over his head.

"Owah! Tagu! Siam!"

His voice got louder with each magic word. When he finished the chant, a tornado of magical golden light swirled around him, growing larger and larger.

Boom! The light exploded, blowing off the roof of the library tower.

The monsters vanished. Jestro and The Book of Monsters went hurtling through the windows and out of the castle. Outside the library door, the vibrations of the explosion knocked Clay out cold.

When he woke up, the other knights were gathered around him.

"Wh-what happened?" Clay asked.

"You tell us, buddy," said Aaron.

Clay got up and forced open the library door. All of the books had been sent flying in the explosion. Stray pages floated in the air like birds.

"Must be the maid's day off," joked Lance.

Then Clay saw it—Merlok's hat, still glowing with scorch marks from the explosion.

The wizard was nowhere in sight.

"Merlok's gone!" Clay cried. "It was Jestro and he had monsters and a magical book. And he was going to crush us!"

"Jestro? What's wrong with him?" asked Macy.

"He's always been more than a little out there," said Lance.

Clay fell to his knees. "Merlok used some big spell and . . . *boom.* I couldn't save him. I was helpless. I . . . I don't deserve to be a knight."

"Don't blame yourself, Clay," Macy said, trying to console him. "None of us are ready for whatever this is."

"We'd better be," said Clay. "And fast!"

40

CHAPTER 7

Clay took a deep breath. He knew he had to stay calm. He told the knights everything he could remember about the monsters he had seen. He explained how Merlok had saved him—and sacrificed himself.

He picked up the battered hat. "I still can't believe he's gone," said Clay. "I'm a knight. I should be saving people. Maybe I don't deserve my shield."

Macy put a comforting hand on his shoulder.

In the castle's computer room, Ava was frantically typing on the main console to try to repair the castle's electronic systems.

Robin walked in. "The Squirebots are getting the power back on all over Knighton. It shouldn't take long."

Ava nodded, but she was frowning. "The power failure totally fried the servers. I've got to find a way to get the castle grid up and running."

The digital blue holo screens were up working, but Ava hadn't been able to get any of the programs to function. Then, without warning, one of the screens began to glow and hum.

"Looks like you did something," Robin said.

"Can't take credit for this," Ava told him.

A mechanical voice came from the screen. "Je-je-je-jes-tro . . ."

"Wait, what was that?" Ava asked. "Jestro?"

At that moment, the jester was walking through the dark forest, carrying The Book of Monsters. They had both survived the blast, but they looked a little battered.

"I can't believe we got blown up," Jestro complained. "I mean, look at me! I'm a wreck. This is awful. How long have we been walking?"

"Ten minutes, bad boy," The Book of Monsters replied.

"That long?" asked Jestro.

"Moan, moan, moan," the book teased. "You're the most delicate evil jester I've ever met. You need to stay focused on your revenge."

"You're getting heavy," Jestro said. "You're a pretty fat book."

He stopped and set the book down on a tree stump.

"I'm not fat, I just have big binding!" the book protested. But he knew that Jestro couldn't go on carrying him forever. "Okay, open to page three and get out the Book Keeper."

Jestro cautiously opened the book. "I'm not too sure about this. The last time I tried this I got blasted across the kingdom."

"Oh, don't be such a baby," snapped the book.

Jestro waved the staff over the page and a streak of purple light shot from the book. The light transformed into a small creature. About half as tall as Jestro, the monster was red, with black hair and one yellow eye larger than the other.

Jestro backed away nervously. The little monster walked over to the book, shut it, and hoisted it into his arms. Then he tottered over to Jestro.

"See?" the book said. "Now this little Book Keeper can carry me around. Happy?"

"Fine, but who's going to carry *me*?" Jestro whined.

"Look, you kooky clown! I told you, I'd make you into the best evil force this realm has ever seen, so stop all your complaining or I'm out. Book Keeper, turn me around! I don't want to look at him."

The Book Keeper turned the book around—all the way around, in a complete circle, so that the book was face-to-face with Jestro again.

"No, no! Turn me halfway around! I'm turning my back cover on him!"

The Book Keeper did it right this time.

"All right," said Jestro. "I'll stop moaning. Now tell me again, what's the plan?"

The Book of Monsters outlined his wicked plot.

"It's simple," he said. "We hunt down those evil books that magic Mer-loser blasted all over the kingdom. The more evil books we get, the more evil we'll be."

"You mean the more evil *I'll* be, right?" asked Jestro.

"Yeah, yeah, right. Now let's go." He sniffed the air. "I smell nasty."

"Actually, you do have a pretty musty odor," Jestro said.

The book got defensive. "I've been on a shelf for a hundred years! Without any deodorant!"

Then the three of them headed farther into the dark, spooky forest.

CHAPTER 8

Inside the Joustdome, Squirebots worked to try to restore power. Others were cleaning up after the Graduation Battle-bration.

Macy walked into the training room and found Clay angrily hacking a wooden target to pieces with his sword.

"Clay, we need a plan. We need to be ready for anything," she told him.

"I know," Clay said, not taking his eyes off his next target. "I think better when I'm training."

He threw a broken piece of target in the air and jumped up to reach it.

Whack! He sliced it right in two.

Nearby, Lane was facedown on a massage table as a Squirebot karate-chopped his back.

"A little to the left, Dennis," Lance instructed.

Clay glared at Lance. With a cry, he angrily hurled his sword at a target just above Dennis's head. The sword hit the bull's-eye, and the Squirebot ran away, screaming.

Lance looked up. "Hey! You ruined my midday massage."

Clay marched up to Lance. "Most of the city's without power! Merlok is gone! Dark magic may be loose! You realize we're dealing with epic, life-altering events here?"

"Of course. You know how tense I am right now?" Lance asked, sitting up. "I have a knot in my shoulder the size of a grapefruit."

"I don't have time to massage your ego. We need to train!" Clay said.

In one swift motion, he pulled the sword out of the target and sliced through the legs of the massage table. Lance jumped off as the broken table clattered to the floor.

Angry now, Lance pressed a button on the handle of his lance. The pole slid out and he charged toward Clay.

Clang! Metal clashed against metal as the lance and the sword hit each other.

"Who put you in charge?" Lance asked. "You're not the boss of me."

Clang! Clang! Clang!

"I'm the only one here who truly lives by the Knights' Code!" Clay replied as the two traded blows.

Clang! Clang!

"Boys! This is totally unproductive," Macy said, but Lance and Clay ignored her and kept battling.

"Axl! A little help here!" Macy called out.

Axl gulped down the last bite of the chicken leg he was eating and came over. He picked up Clay in one hand and Lance in the other.

"Come on, guys, you're giving me an upset stomach," Axl said.

Clang! The two knights kept fighting, even though their feet were dangling above the floor.

"I see you had to call reinforcements. Not something a *true* leader would do," Lance told Clay.

"At least I'm not lying around rubbing people the wrong way!" Clay shot back.

Macy sighed, shook her head, and left the training room. Those two were hopeless!

Over in the castle, Robin and Ava were busy at work in the computer room. Robin had just attached radar dish helmets to five Squirebots.

"Radar helmets check out," he said. "Now what?"

Ava called up an image of Knightonia on her screen. "Put these guys in strategic locations around the city and we can triangulate the origin of that weird signal we got earlier," she replied.

"Ready!" the Squirebots said excitedly. They turned on their radar helmets, then headed out to locate the signal.

CHAPTER 9

The Book of Monsters sniffed the air as the Book Keeper moved him through the dark forest. Jestro followed behind them. He kept waving his staff in the air and making weird faces.

"What are you doing? Other than being annoying?" the book asked him.

"I'm practicing my evil poses," Jestro replied. "You said practice makes perfect."

"I mean practice being *actually* bad, not a poser," said the book. "You need to be ready to use me to call forth nasty, awful monsters."

"Okay," said Jestro. Then he moved away and turned back again, snarling and waving

52

his arms in the air. "How about this one? Haaaa!"

The Book of Monsters rolled his eyes. "Oh, I am terrified," he said in a voice that proved he clearly wasn't. "You make me want to cry for my mommy, Jestro the Evil."

Jestro nodded. "Jestro the Evil? I like the sound of that!"

The book sniffed the air again. "Hey, I smell something! It's that way."

The Book Keeper ran off with The Book of Monsters.

"No, the *other* way!" cried the book.

The Book Keeper changed direction.

"Oh yeah!" said the book, sniffing again. "I smell a magic book nearby. And it smells *bad*."

Jestro looked around nervously as they walked deeper into the forest. Even though it was morning, no sunlight came through the trees here. No birds sang. He shivered.

Then a white rabbit hopped toward him. Jestro was relieved to see something so cute in this gloomy place.

"Look, it's a harmless little bunny!" he said, reaching toward it.

The bunny's eyes turned red and it growled, revealed sharp fangs. Jestro backed away in fear. "*Ahh!* That's the most vicious rodent I've ever set eyes on!" he yelled.

"I know why," said The Book of Monsters. "Look! The Book of Evil!"

There, lodged in the dirt, was a book with a purple cover adorned with a glowing yellow symbol.

"It doesn't look so bad," Jestro said.

He picked it up—and black ooze crawled out of it into his hands, and then spread over his body. His costume changed from purple and blue to dark blue and red. A strange yellow glow came over his eyes. The points on his jester hat curled up to look like horns.

"Quick! Quick! Feed me!" cried The Book of Monsters.

Jestro tossed The Book of Evil to The Book of Monsters. He caught it in his mouth and greedily chewed and swallowed it down.

"Let's party!" yelled The Book of Monsters with an evil cackle.

Back in the castle, Ava studied the map of the city. The Squirebots with radar helmets showed up as blinking dots.

Robin's face popped up on the screen. "That's the last radar Squirebot. How's it look?" he asked her.

"Great," she replied. "Grid is set, five-by-five."

Macy walked in. "Radar Squirebots? What are you guys doing?"

"Trying to restore the castle's operating systems and power," Ava answered. "But we've been getting weird messages."

"Messages?" Macy asked.

Suddenly, Ava's computer screen flickered. Lights flashed. A blurry shape appeared on the screen.

Then a voice crackled from the screen. "Jes . . . Att . . . Castle . . . Jes . . . tro."

"There it is!" Ava cried. Then she frowned. "I can't locate it."

"Who is it?" Macy asked. "What do they want?"

The screen flickered, and then it went dark.

"It's gone," Ava said. "But I may have gotten a fix on the Wi-Fi source."

Macy looked worried. "What's going on?" she wondered.

Early the next morning, the knights returned to the training room in the Joustdome. Aaron zipped around the room on his hover shield, doing flips and other tricks. He hovered in the air next to Axl, whose shield was piled high with food.

"This Knightronic Shield is the best hover-board I've ever had," Aaron reported.

"Mine works best as a plate," said Axl. He brought the shield to his open mouth, tipped the food inside, and swallowed it in one gulp. Then he let out a loud burp.

Nearby, Clay and Lance were *still* trading blows with their weapons.

"Respect the Knights' Code," said Clay as his sword clanked weakly against Lance's shield.

"Respect my nap time," said Lance, stifling a yawn.

He swept at Clay with his lance, and the two knights fell into each other, exhausted.

"You take nothing seriously," said Clay.

"And you're super bossy," Lance countered.

Macy entered and looked around the room. Aaron was doing tricks on his hover shield, Axl was eating, and Clay and Lance looked like they had been fighting each other all night. She shook her head.

How were they supposed to battle monsters if they couldn't work together and come up with a plan?

CHAPTER 10

Let's make some monsters!" Jestro cried.

"Some evil, nasty monsters!" agreed The Book of Monsters. He could feel the power from The Book of Evil flowing through him.

Jestro threw open the book. On every page, monsters moved and called to them, anxious to get out.

Jestro waved his wand over the open pages. "Nasty, evil monsters, come forth and serve me! Make the folks around us wet their pants and flee!"

Globlins, Bloblins, and Scurriers bounced out of the book, cackling and laughing.

"How great is this?" Jestro asked. "More!"

He waved his staff again, and two huge monsters appeared. One was Sparkks, the one-eyed giant who had been released in the library. The second was just as tall as Sparkks, with a body glowing fiery red; a mouth full of nasty teeth; two glowing, yellow eyes; and a gray, curved horn on each side of his head.

"Burnzie and Sparkks, ready to serve you," the two monsters said.

"Excellent!" said Jestro. "I'll have a tuna on rye with a pickle and coleslaw."

"To serve your plan for evil vengeance, joke-boy!" The Book of Monsters snarled. "They're horrible monsters, not waiters."

"Right," said Jestro. "Then let's go hassle those jerks in the castle!"

In the castle, the knights didn't know that a monster army was on its way to attack them. Clay was working out with a bench press, lifting a metal pole with a Squirebot hanging on each end.

"I agree with you, Macy," Clay was saying. "We should be training and ready for everything."

Lance and Axl were playing a video game.

"You guys worry too much," said Lance.

Macy shook her head. "We need to get organized and get out there and be knights."

"Woo-hoo!"

Aaron whizzed by on his hover shield and grabbed Macy by the arm, taking her with him.

"You've tried all day to get everyone organized, Macy," he said as they flew around the training room. "Maybe you just let them . . . chill."

"Chill? Just chill, Aaron?" Macy asked angrily. She hopped onto the hover shield and turned to face him. "The kingdom needs us. My father needs us. Whoa!"

They crashed into a stack of boxes. Macy tumbled off the board and tossed a box that had landed on her head. She sighed. "And I want to prove to him so badly that I can be a knight."

Aaron sat down next to her. "I get it. You'll get your chance."

"Yeah, but when?" Macy asked.

Whaa! Whaa! Whaa! An alarm rang through the Joustdome, and a red light flashed.

"Uh, sooner than you think?" Aaron asked.

As the knights raced to gear up for battle, Jestro and The Book of Monsters approached the castle with their army of monsters.

"I feel . . . a little queasy," Jestro said. Even though he was trying to be evil, the idea of attacking the castle didn't feel right to him.

"Don't barf on me," snapped the book. "Just remember: This is your chance to get back at all those people who laughed at you. Who think you're nothing but a joke."

Jestro closed his eyes and remembered everyone laughing and pointing at him. He opened them again, and his eyes were blazing.

"It's time to attack!" he yelled.

The Book of Monsters grinned. "He's *baaaack*, and he's *baaaad*!" he cheered. "Time to take down that castle!"

"Burnzie and Sparkks, fling 'em!" ordered Jestro.

The two big monsters scooped up Globlins and hurled them at the castle. They flew over the walls of the castle and landed on the royal balcony.

Two Squirebots leapt in front of the king and queen, their swords raised.

"Protect the king!" yelled one.

"Protect the queen!" yelled the other.

Bop! Bop! Bop! The Globlins knocked them both down.

"It's an invasion!" the king cried.

The castle gates opened and a squad of Squirebots ran out to try to stop the Globlin onslaught. They trembled when they saw Burnzie and Sparkks, but they bravely faced them.

"Hold your ground!" ordered their leader.

Whomp! Burnzie reached down and tossed them aside, leaving only the leader. The Squirebot raised his sword.

"Have at you!" he cried.

Burnzie breathed on the sword, and it glowed with red-hot heat. The Squirebot dropped it and ran away, screaming.

Laughing, Burnzie picked up a Globlin and rolled it toward an advancing squad of Squirebots. The Globlin slammed into the first one, and the rest of them toppled over like bowling pins.

Sparkks laughed. "Yes!" he cried, high-fiving Burnzie.

Then the castle gates opened again. This time, it revealed the five knights, ready for

battle! Their shields and weapons were glowing with power.

"Time to show everyone that we deserved
to graduate from the Knights' Academy!"
said Clay.

CHAPTER 11

Okay knights, let's hit them on the right flank," Clay said.

The five knights charged forward.

Clay jumped up and kicked Sparkks in the head. Then he landed on the opposite side of the monster. Sparkks turned around and aimed a punch at Clay. Clay dodged it, and the monster's fist hit the road and broke the concrete.

Clay jumped up to attack Sparkks again, but this time the monster's fist hit its mark. Clay fell backward with a thud.

Lance stood over him, grinning.

"You deal with monsters your way, I'll deal with monsters my way," he said.

He charged at Burnzie with his lance extended. Burnzie grabbed the weapon and lifted Lance off the ground.

"Puny knight," he taunted, and then tossed Lance aside. He landed next to Clay and gave him a sheepish grin.

Aaron flew around the courtyard on his hover shield.

"Here comes the stick!" he cried, shooting at Globlins with his crossbow. Blue energy arrows shot out and hit their targets— but the arrows just bounced off the Globlins!

Macy wasn't having any luck, either. She pounded at the Globlins with her mace, but they kept popping right back.

"I hate these hot little things!" she complained.

Axl swatted at the Globlins with his battle-axe.

"Get off me!" he growled as a swarm of them piled on him.

Jestro and The Book of Monsters advanced toward the battle zone.

"The knights," said Jestro anxiously.

"They're nothing!" said The Book of Monsters. "You wiped the floor with that Moorington guy."

"But Clay was always good to me," Jestro said.

"Don't go soft on me!" the book snapped. "He still let people laugh and laugh. They *all* laughed at you."

Up in the royal balcony, a Globlin came flying toward King Halbert. Queen Halbert jumped up and kicked it away.

"Lay off my king!" she said angrily.

More Globlins flew toward the balcony, and the queen grabbed the nearest weapon she could find—a Squirebot. She picked him up and used him as a baseball bat to knock away the little red monsters.

Down below, the knights did their best to

protect the castle gates, but the monsters kept yelling.

"Hold them off! Hold them off!" Clay yelled.

Lance batted away Globlins with his lance, but they kept bouncing back.

"Crazy burning blobs!" he yelled. "These weapons have almost no effect on these monsters."

"And you've got the best weapons money can buy," Macy remarked as she smacked two Globlins with her mace.

"I know, right?" Lance replied.

"We've got to get organized," Macy said. "We're being overrun!"

Clay jumped and landed next to her. "Just keep fighting!" he said, hitting two Globlins with his sword.

The Globlins just kept coming and coming. They swarmed Axl until he couldn't fight them off anymore. They knocked him down and bounced on his armor.

"I've decided I don't like monsters," he announced.

Aaron zipped up on his hover shield. "They don't like you either, big guy!" he said. He shot at the Globlins with his energy arrows.

The Book of Monsters grinned at Jestro. "I told you they'd be no match for you and your monsters."

Jestro laughed with glee. "I'm good at something!" he cried happily. Then his smile turned into an evil snarl. "I'm good at being bad!"

In another part of the castle, Ava and Robin followed a radar Squirebot into Merlok's library.

"I finally locked onto it," Ava said. "This is the source of that mysterious signal."

"Here?" asked Robin. "This place has been blasted to bits."

Ava walked over to the computer console and turned it on. A blue holographic screen appeared in front of her. She quickly typed on the keyboard. The blue screen suddenly turned golden yellow.

"Whoa, power surge," said Robin.

"What's going on?" Ava wondered.

Golden light poured from the screen. It filled the library. Then the light took shape on top of Merlok's desk.

"I am Merlok!" the golden figure cried.

Ava and Robin gasped. The figure of Merlok had appeared on the holographic projector.

"No way! Merlok!" Robin cried. "Well, more like Merlok 2.0."

"Merlok 2.0?" Ava asked. "Really? That sounds like an operating system from twenty years ago." She thought for a moment. "I guess it's better than Merlok Beta, but not by much."

"You're missing the point," Merlok 2.0 said. "I'm here to help you."

"Yeah, now he's like a digital wizard," Robin said. "This is pretty awesome."

"We'll work on the naming thing after we fight some monsters," said Ava.

"Yes!" cheered Merlok 2.0. "Get ready for NEXO Scan!"

Ava quickly patched into Clay's communication system. Clay heard her voice through his shield.

"Clay, it's Ava," she said.

"I'm a little busy right now, Ava," Clay said as he struck Sparkks with a blow from his sword.

"I need you to stop fighting and point your shield to the sky," she said.

"What?" Clay asked.

"Just do it!" Ava said firmly.

Clay did it. He pointed his shield to the sky.

Energy crackled in the air above him, and a holographic golden dragon took shape! The dragon exploded into golden energy that downloaded into Clay's shield, charging it.

"NEXO Power: Dragon of Justice!" Merlok 2.0 yelled.

CHAPTER 12

The power surged through Clay's shield into his sword and armor. Glowing with golden power, he swung at a Globlin. The creature dissolved into a puff of black smoke and then vanished.

"It's Merlok!" Clay realized. He called out to the other knights. "Raise your shields up. Do it!"

Lance, Macy, Aaron, and Axl obeyed. The NEXO Power downloaded into their shields and powered up their weapons and armor, too.

Merlok's voice came through their shields. "Show them the power of the NEXO KNIGHTS heroes!"

Lance's lance sliced through the fiery Globlins.

Poof! They turned into smoke and disappeared.

Macy smashed them with her mace.

Poof! Globlins gone.

Poof! Poof! Poof! Aaron took out the Globlins with his arrows.

Bam! Axl send them packing with his battle-axe.

Jestro looked on in horror.

"What's going on? How are they destroying my monsters?" he asked.

"I ain't The Book of Answers, but I bet that Merlok has something to do with this," guessed The Book of Monsters.

With the Globlins under control, Lance and Clay charged the big monsters.

"Puny monster!" Lance cried, striking Burnzie with his lance.

Sparkks cried out as Clay struck him with his sword.

Both monsters transformed into purple smoke. They flew back into the pages of The Book of Monsters.

"I completely approve of the new Merlok!" said Clay happily.

"Now what?" asked Jestro.

"A new lesson," said The Book of Monsters. "He who fights and runs away, lives to fight another day. Retreat!"

The Book Keeper started to run—right toward the knights!

"No! Retreat the *other* way! The other way, dopey monster!" the book yelled.

The Book Keeper turned and ran away from the castle. Jestro followed. The knights raised their weapons triumphantly.

The battle over, they went to the library to join Robin, Ava, and Merlok 2.0.

Clay looked in wonder at the holographic image of the wizard.

"It's nice to have you back, Merlok," he said.

"I am now Merlok 2.0," corrected the wizard.

"He's a three-dimensional holographic projection now," explained Ava. "He was absorbed into the computer system by his magical blast."

Merlok 2.0 looked at Clay. "Clay, you must prepare," he said. "Jestro will be back and you will face a dire threat from his monsters."

"Where do those creatures come from?" Clay asked.

"That's, well, a long story," Merlok replied.

The king and queen entered the library.

"Merlok, my old friend, it is nice to know that you are still with us," the king said.

"In whatever form you're in," added the queen.

Axl and Aaron picked up two controllers.

"Check this out. He's got a built-in game center," said Aaron.

Little video game knights started marching around Merlok 2.0.

"What's going on?" Merlok 2.0 asked.

"I'm about to get the new high score," said Axl.

"Guys! Guys! You're overloading the circuits!" Ava warned.

"Ahh!" Merlok 2.0 cried. "My digital magic only provides power for—"

The library went dark. The power had gone out once again!

"Darkness has fallen across the land," King Halbert announced.

Macy sighed. "Dad, please. Can somebody find a flashlight?"

Clay laughed. It felt good to have saved the castle from an army of monsters. With the help of Merlok 2.0 and his fellow knights, Clay knew they would be able to defeat any evil that threatened Knighton. Now, if they could just find a light switch . . .

FRIGHT KNIGHT!

Adapted by Kate Howard

SCHOLASTIC INC.

ISBN 978-1-338-11478-2

12 11 10 9 8 7 6 5 4 3 2 1   16 17 18 19 20 21

Printed in the U.S.A.   40

This edition first printing, September 2016

Book design by Rick DeMonico

CONTENTS

FROM THE
FILES OF
MERLOK 2.0

Greetings, and welcome to the Files of Merlok 2.0—that's me! Now where was I . . . Ah, yes! For over one hundred years, the kingdom of Knighton knew only peace. In the capital city of Knightonia, humans and Squirebots began to live side-by-side, surrounded by the city's technical marvels—like the awe-inspiring Beam Bridges or the state-of-the-art Joustdome.

I, Merlok the wizard, used my magic to help the kingdom whenever I could. My greatest task was to keep the dangerous Books of Dark Magic locked away in my library. The most wicked of these books was The Book of Monsters. Under my very nose, this clever book plotted to escape from my library.

One day, the book found the perfect puppet for its plans: Jestro, the court jester. Jestro had no friends in the kingdom except for Clay Moorington. Clay tried to be kind to the jester, but everyone else thought Jestro was a

joke—and not the funny kind. Jestro was tired of everyone laughing at him instead of with him.

Lonely and eager to prove that he was nothing to be laughed at, Jestro was a perfect target for The Book of Monsters' offer. If Jestro freed it, together they could unleash an evil on Knighton. Soon, the citizens of Knighton would be serving Jestro, not laughing at him.

Jestro and The Book of Monsters launched their attack right away. With a wave of a magic staff over the pages of The Book of Monsters, evil monsters sprang to life.

A team of brave knights banded together to fight them. Clay Moorington and his friends Lance Richmond, Macy Halbert, Aaron Fox, and Axl took up their shields and charged against the monsters. But muscle and iron are no match against magic monsters.

In the end, I was the only one who could stop them. I cast a powerful magic spell to destroy

the monsters and . . . *boom!* Jestro
and The Book of Monsters were blown
far away from the castle. Although
the monsters were defeated, my
library was also destroyed, and
dangerous Books of Evil were
scattered across the kingdom.

The explosion also left me
trapped as a digital hologram in
the castle's computer system. But
it isn't all bad. Now, I am able to
harness the power of magic and
technology together. In this new
form I can download magical NEXO
Powers to the knights, so they can
defeat whatever monsters attack.

Now it's a fair fight. Clay,
Lance, Macy, Aaron, and Axl train
with their NEXO Weapons and NEXO
Shields so they'll always be ready
when Jestro and The Book of
Monsters attack—and they will! The
NEXO KNIGHTS team has only just
begun to see what Jestro's monsters
can do . . .

CHAPTER 1

The sun was setting when the NEXO KNIGHTS team's rolling castle—the Fortrex—rumbled up to the village of Spittoon. The sky was awash in bright orange and pink streaks, making the village look peaceful and welcoming. But the knights of Avatron knew looks could be deceiving. There were dark powers at work in their usually peaceful land—specifically, Jestro, the court's former jester, and an ancient Book of Monsters. Jestro was using the book to release monsters all over the kingdom. So these five new graduates of the Knights'

Academy were on a quest to try to bring peace and safety back to the Realm of Knighton.

"I sense a great power near the rough-and-tumble town of Spittoon," said Merlok 2.0 from inside his operating system. Once a powerful wizard (with a seriously snazzy wizard's beard, hat, swishy cloak, and the rest of the look), Merlok had recently gotten sucked into a computer. Now, he existed as a complicated computer program—with some pretty cool digi-magic at his disposal.

Merlok 2.0 was only just getting used to his new powers . . . and his new look. As part of the Fortrex's computer system, Merlok 2.0 was now a bright-orange hologram. With his digi-magic, he was able to help the NEXO KNIGHTS team when they most needed it. He could download NEXO Powers right into their armor. If they needed a specific kind of help during

a battle, they could summon Merlok's help and—*ka-pow!*—instant digi-magic fighting powers!

Merlok 2.0 breathed deeply. Though he couldn't actually smell anything from inside his computerized shell, he knew deep breaths and a calm voice always made a person seem wiser. Deep breath in, deep sigh out. The digital wizard's voice rang out over the Fortrex's operating system as he scanned the village in front of their rolling castle. "I can feel the power surrounding Spittoon in my ancient bones."

Clay Moorington—the most knightly of all the NEXO KNIGHTS heroes—gazed out from the highest tower of the Fortrex. Clay adjusted his blue-and-gold armor and puffed out his chest. "Spittoon is the toughest village in the Realm," he told Merlok 2.0 and Lance Richmond, his fellow knight.

"They spit a lot," Lance noted casually. "It's unsanitary."

Clay ignored the useless information as he squinted out over the village of Spittoon. Lance never took things seriously enough for a true knight, and it frustrated Clay. The Knights' Code told Clay that he must consider their next move carefully. He wished he wasn't the only one in the group who worried about the impression he and the other knights were making on the people of the Realm. Because they had just graduated from the Knights' Academy, the five NEXO KNIGHTS heroes still had a long way to go before they had fully earned the trust and respect of the people of the Realm.

"We're gonna have to make an entrance that impresses them," Clay said. He had a feeling Lance would like this idea—handsome,

4

popular Lance loved nothing more than to make a grand entrance. And because he was the most famous of the knights, Lance absolutely loved being noticed.

Clay turned and spoke to a group of mechanical Squirebots who were anxiously awaiting their orders. "Squires, play the 'Fanfare of Fortitude.'" On his command, the band of Squirebots—who called themselves The Boogie Knights—played a regal song. As the music washed over the valley, Clay turned to address the people of Spittoon. "Greetings, citizens of Spittoon! We are the Knights of Knighton, sworn protectors of the Realm."

The people who were gathered below looked up. For a moment, it almost seemed like they were cowering in fear. Then it was clear that they *were* cowering in fear. At the

sound of Clay's voice, many of Spittoon's villagers scattered and ran for cover. Inside their homes, the citizens shuttered their windows and doors.

"They seem a bit, um . . . skittish," Merlock 2.0 said.

Lance yawned, then shot Clay an amused smile. "See? You scared them with your boringness, Clay."

"This is supposed to be the toughest village in the Realm?" Clay scoffed.

"Times change," Lance told him. He shrugged arrogantly and added, "You gotta change with them." He nodded at the musical Squirebots. Wiggling his eyebrows, he ordered, "Put a little funk in that fanfare, will ya?"

The Boogie Knights cranked up the funk factor. The band of robots danced and

swayed as they blasted their trumpets and lutes.

"Lance," Clay growled. This was not a time for nonsense! "What are you doing?"

Lance shrugged. He knew it would all work out—eventually. When you were Lance, things always did. "I'm working on our entrance, Clay-man. You only get one chance to make a first impression, you know."

"Yes, I do." Clay held out his hand to silence The Boogie Knights' trumpet section. "Which is why I hoped—as per our Knights' Code—we would present ourselves with power, respect, and solemn dignity."

Aaron Fox burst out onto the balcony just in time to add, "And no fear!" The most daring of the knights zoomed past the others. Aaron often used his shield as a hoverboard, which really ruffled Clay's armor

(Clay wished his fellow knight would realize his shield was *not* a toy!).

With a twist and a backflip, Aaron leapt onto his hover shield and dropped off the side of the balcony tower. Whooping, Aaron blasted away from the Fortrex and soared toward the houses that lined the quiet streets of Spittoon. His snazzy green-and-gray armor was a streak of color in the darkening sky.

As Aaron raced toward the village, the town roared to life. Many of the villagers who hadn't already hidden away inside their homes screamed and ducked for cover. Aaron zoomed over the tops of houses, his hover shield skimming across rooftops before it delivered him into the center of the village.

Clay watched the mayhem from above. Suddenly, he realized Aaron wasn't the only

one of the knights who had ventured out into Spittoon. Axl, the largest—and hungriest—of the knights had also made his way into the town's center. The enormous knight lumbered through the town like a gentle giant, but the villagers ran from him like he was an ogre! Clay watched him from above, then called out, "Axl!"

But Axl was too distracted by a food cart. As Clay watched on from the Fortrex, Axl grabbed a chunk of meat from the vendor's stand. "Boring?" Axl grunted, drooling over the meat. "BOAR-ing!" He gobbled up the chunk of boar in one bite, hardly noticing that the shopkeeper had jumped up and fled when he saw Axl coming. "Yum!" Axl said happily, munching loudly.

"Why are they all so afraid of everything?" Clay wondered aloud as the people of

Spittoon scattered. "They should be spitting and grunting and scratching themselves, if memory serves. What do you think, Merlok? Lance?" He turned. Neither the wizard nor Lance was on the balcony with him any-more. "Merlok? Lance?!" Clay peered over the tower wall again.

In town, Lance had managed to find a pack of Squirazzi and a few adoring fans. Lance posed and preened, waiting for the usual happy screams. He *loved* being such a popular guy. Lance blew air kisses at the crowd, waving majestically. But instead of cheering and clapping, the crowds around him fled. They screamed with terror.

"Wow," Lance said, brushing his hair away from his face. "Something really is weird here."

Clay looked around, realizing he was alone—with only The Boogie Knights for

backup—at the top of the tower. He shrugged at the band and said, "You might as well go down there, too. Just as long as you take—" But before he could finish his orders, the Squirebots leaped over the edge of the wall and slid into Spittoon. Clay sighed. "...As long as you take the stairs."

The Boogie Knights crashed at the bottom, landing in a tumbled heap of instruments. Clay was furious. Why was he the only one who took this job seriously?! "Does anybody remember our plan to make a 'respectful, dignified' entrance?"

"I do, Clay," said Macy Halbert. She strutted out onto the balcony and gazed out over Spittoon. As the king's daughter, Macy understood the words respectful and dignified better than anyone...she just didn't *enjoy* being respectful and dignified when it meant she couldn't also be rough and

tumble. Macy wanted nothing more than to have some fierce fun once in a while! "Watch this—and this!" Macy swung her mace around her head, pretending she was deep in battle. Her red ponytail swung through the air as she whipped her powerful weapon around and around. "And some of this!" Macy grunted and swung, eager to impress her fellow knight with her toughness.

"All I can say is..." Clay broke off suddenly. "Oh no!" Below them, a small child was standing on the edge of a well. She had her arms outstretched, trying to grab a balloon that had escaped from her chubby fingers. The hairs on the back of Clay's neck stood up. It looked like a citizen was in danger— and that meant it was time for a real hero to take action! With a powerful jump, Clay leapt over the edge of the castle wall and slid into the village. He whisked the child out

of harm's way just before she toppled into the well.

"Now *that* was awesome!" Aaron cheered. He leaned against his hover shield and cheered. "What's Lance talkin' about? You *totally* know how to make an entrance, Clay!"

"I wasn't 'making an entrance,'" Clay huffed. "I was saving this young damsel in distress." He smiled down at the little girl, patting her head gently. "Now run along, little girl. Oh . . . and don't forget your balloon!" He held out the girl's balloon, expecting her to thank him with a grateful smile.

But instead, the girl's mother rushed forward and grabbed her daughter away from the pack of gathered knights. "My baby!" she screeched. "My baby! My baby!"

As the mother and child raced away from the knights, Aaron shrugged one shoulder. Then he reached forward and popped the

balloon with a cheeky grin. The few remaining villagers who hadn't yet gone into hiding screamed when they heard the sound of the popping balloon. Then they fled, too. Within seconds, the entire town center was deserted. The knights were alone.

Clay was totally stumped. He couldn't understand why everyone in the town was running from them in fear. Turning to his fellow knights, Clay asked, "*What* is going on here?!"

The five knights returned to the Fortrex Command Center to discuss the situation with Merlok 2.0. The team's two knights-in-training, Ava and Robin, joined them. Ava and Robin were on a break from their first year at the Knights' Academy. The two junior knights helped the team with tech

and computer support when they were out on their missions, hoping someday they would get to join the NEXO KNIGHTS team, too.

The hologram of Merlok 2.0 spoke to all of them all in a serious voice, "Sorcery is going on here."

The knights gazed into their view-screen image of the village. The streets were all still empty, except for one lone villager who was peeking out his front door. When Axl burped—loudly, so it echoed through the valley—the villager jumped and slammed his door closed again.

"So much for a tough town," Lance said, rolling his eyes.

Ava punched a few buttons on the computer, pulling up a screen with a bunch of graphs. "Whoa," she murmured, her eyes

flickering across the screen. "Some of these readings are off the chart. What's going on?"

"It's just as I suspected," Merlok 2.0 said ominously. "There is a Book of Magic. Somewhere in the Dark Woods. It is very powerful. And *very* scary. We need to get this evil book away from the village . . . or Spittoon will be lost to fear forever."

16

CHAPTER 2

Deep in the Dark Woods, Jestro—the King's seriously unfunny court jester—was plotting with his new-found evil mentor: The Book of Monsters. Now, The Book of Monsters was no ordinary book. It could talk (too much, Jestro thought), scheme (very well, Jestro admitted), and was filled with dark, magical power. With the right spell, the caster could make evil creatures from the book's pages come to life.

But the knights had already defeated Jestro and the book's monsters before. The villains needed to make their monsters

stronger, and there was only one way to do that. They had to find the eleven powerful Books of Dark Magic scattered across the Realm and feed them to The Book of Monsters. By eating the magical books, The Book of Monsters would become even more power-ful and release some extra-special creeps.

Now, in the Dark Woods, Jestro had stum-bled across a new book. And this one looked deliciously sinister.

"Watch it, clown-boy," The Book of Monsters warned as Jestro poked at the mysterious, glowing book with two sticks. "You gotta be very careful. You *don't* want to touch . . . *The Book of Fear*!"

"Yeah, yeah," Jestro muttered. He fur-rowed his brow as he tried to lift The Book of Fear to get a better look. The jester's painted-on smiley face looked shadowy and cruel in

the dark forest. "So it's a spooky book. All I care about is that we beat those goody knights to it." He thrust the creepy book at The Book of Monsters, urging it to gobble it up. "Just open wide and . . . down the hatch."

The Book of Monsters sputtered, "Hey, wait . . . hold—" But Jestro had already shoved The Book of Fear into its mouth. The Book of Monsters chewed it up. Jestro laughed and waved his staff over The Book of Monsters' open pages. "Let's see what kind of monsters this gets us!"

The Book of Monsters burped. Purple smoke filled the air as The Book of Monsters shuddered and glowed. A moment later, three glowing Globlins popped out of The Book of Monsters' pages. All three of the evil flaming-red balls sprouted spider legs, then scurried around the dark forest.

They were ready to work their magic fear-power.

The Book of Monsters continued to shake and glow. More purple smoke filled the air. Then a moment later, another ominous creature popped out of the book's pages. She was tall and glowed like hot coals, with a long serpent's tail that slithered across the forest floor. The creature hissed, then flicked a pair of fiery whips into the air. Jestro had never seen anything like her before. She was so terrifying that he took a cautious step backward and hid behind a giant rock.

"Hey, scaredy-pants," The Book of Monsters teased Jestro. "Don't worry about Whiparella here. As long as her whips don't touch you, you'll be fine." Whiparella snapped her shimmering whips all around, narrowly missing Jestro's clownish face.

Jestro shrieked in fear, then tried to act cool about it.

"And that hair!" The Book of Monsters said, gazing at Whiparella. "Love it! Isn't she frightening?"

"Uh, yeah," Jestro agreed. "She's plenty scary. Not to me, obviously, but I can see how she would fill others with fear." He grinned mischievously. He had been look-ing for just the right creature to torture the NEXO KNIGHTS team. Giggling, Jestro said, "Like those pesky knights! Finally, they will know real fear!"

Nearby, the NEXO KNIGHTS team forged into the Dark Woods on their new quest. They were on the hunt for the powerful book Merlok 2.0 had warned them about. They had no idea Jestro had already found it

and summoned some seriously frightful monsters.

"Hey," Macy said, glancing around at the creepy trees surrounding them. Rocks cast shadows over the dark ground, and branches drooped close over their heads. "Do you think we should wait until morning to look for this book?"

"You heard Merlok," Clay said. "We've got to get that thing before Jestro does."

"Why do you wanna wait, Macy?" Aaron teased. "Are you scared?" Aaron and the three other guys chuckled.

Macy scoffed, "No, I'm not *scared*. I just think it would be easier to see in the *Dark* Woods when it's *light* out."

"She sounds scared to me," Lance noted. The other three laughed again.

"Fear not, Macy," Clay said nobly. "There is nothing out here that can frighten us."

In the dark and gloomy forest, none of the knights noticed that Whiparella had slipped out of the shadows. Slowly, quietly, she crept past the knights. Then, with a quick flick of her wrist, she shot one of her whips out and grabbed Clay around the ankle. Tugging with a silent stealth, she pulled him into the forest with her.

"Clay!" Macy shouted when she realized their friend was gone. The four remaining knights skidded to a stop and spun around, searching through the shadows for some sign of Clay. But just like Macy had told them all, it was too dark.

Clay was nowhere to be seen.

"What happened?" Clay moaned when he came to a few minutes later. His eyes were glassy as he gazed into the thick forest. He blinked, unable to clear away all of the

magical purple haze that clouded his vision. "Feels like something stung me . . ."

Whiparella smirked from the trees while she watched her magic take hold. Whenever her whips touched someone, that person was overcome with his or her own worst nightmares. Whiparella could figure out her victims' biggest fears and bring them to life! She was cooking up something truly fun for Clay . . .

Clay's eyes focused on the forest around him. He blinked. Then again, finally clearing the purple haze away. He looked into the trees, sure he had seen something strange. Was that—?

"Help!" A woman cried from nearby. As Clay watched, the woman was snatched up and carried away through the forest by a monster! From atop the monster's shoulders, the woman screeched in fear.

Clay leapt to his feet. It was time for him to take action! "Fear not, ma'am! I, Clay Moorington, Knight of Knighton, shall assist you in this dark wood!" He puffed out his chest. He flexed his biceps. He brushed off his armor. He did everything he could to make himself look as knightly as a true knight should.

The damsel rolled her eyes. "Will you just hurry up and save me already? This damsel is in some serious distress!"

Clay charged into the forest—and farther away from the rest of the knights. When there was a damsel to rescue, *nothing* could stand in his way. He raced through the forest, ducking under branches.

"Hurry, brave knight!" The damsel called out. "My captor is getting weary! It shall be with great ease that you do your knight's duty and rescue me now."

"For Justice!" Clay bellowed. "For Honor! For a damsel!" He raced forward. "There, m'lady! The monster has ... gotten away?" He scratched his head and looked around. There was no sign of the damsel in distress *or* her captor. How had they escaped him?

A cry came from deeper in the forest. "Help!"

Clay was stumped. He had *never* failed in a rescue mission. And he certainly wasn't about to now. He scratched his chin, perplexed.

Nearby, Jestro and The Book of Monsters watched Clay with great delight. They knew that with Whiparella's magic at work, Clay would *never* save this damsel. And it was going to be great fun to watch his torture. "Oh, yeah!" The Book of Monsters said, laughing. "She found his fear!"

CHAPTER 3

Is it time to eat yet?" Axl asked, sniffing a stick to see if it smelled like food. The enormous knight poked under a large leaf, looking for any sign of Clay . . . and snacks.

Aaron groaned. "You just had third breakfast."

"Sorry, Axl," Lance told him. "First we find Clay, then we break for, um, first lunch." He headed off into the forest.

Macy called after him, "But I heard something over here." She pointed in the opposite direction.

"Perhaps we should split up," Lance suggested.

"In the Dark Woods?" Macy gasped.

"What . . . are you scared?" Aaron teased.

Macy shook her head. "No, of course not. I'm just saying we should, uh . . . split up and find Clay."

"Great idea," Lance muttered. "Wish *I'd* thought of that."

The knights all set off in different directions. After walking only a short distance, Axl tipped his head up and sniffed. His nose had caught a whiff of something delicious. But a moment later, Whiparella's whip hit him and Axl was overtaken with The Book of Fear's powers. His eyes glowed purple as the magic set in. "*Mmm*. Something smells good."

He had no idea Whiparella was lurking in

the bushes nearby, and that what he smelled was all just a trick to torture him . . .

Axl followed his nose to a large dinner table that was heaped with food and drinks in the middle of the forest. "So much food!" Axl grunted, his mouth watering. He rushed toward the table, ready to chow down. But just before he got to it, a gang of flaming Globlins shot out of the woods and devoured every last scrap of food on the table. There was nothing left but dirty dishes. It was Axl's worst nightmare—no food! "Noooooo!" he screamed.

Nearby, Jestro and The Book of Monsters watched the scene with great delight. Jestro giggled. "What a big fraidy cat," he said.

Elsewhere in the woods, Lance strutted proudly. He whistled and kept his shoulders

back. He hoped that by trying to look relaxed, he might begin to feel a bit less tense, too. He peeked between two leaves—and got a brief glimpse of Whiparella's glowing whips. He scratched his head, curious about what he had seen . . .

But before he could figure it out, Whiparella snapped her whips at him. She was eager to overpower Lance with her cruel magic. He was hit. Lance swooned.

"Hey, bugs," Lance called out, feeling woozy as Whiparella's magic seeped into him. "Don't bite me . . . I'm a Richmond!" He spun around, but Whiparella had already slipped away, sight unseen. Lance's eyes went fuzzy and glowed purple with the book's magic.

Then a moment later, he brightened. Ahead of him in the forest he spotted Burnzie

the monster. The enormous red beast was surrounded by a pack of Squirazzi! The Squirazzi's cameras were flashing like crazy, taking picture after picture of the big, foolish monster. Burnzie grinned and the monster's grotesque teeth glowed white with each flash of the camera.

"Hey!" Lance called out. Cameras always *loved* him. This would be the perfect opportunity for the Squirazzi to catch Lance acting like a true hero. His bravery would be captured on film, and he would be even *more* of a star than he already was! He would certainly be known from now on as the most *famous*, most *brave* knight in all the Realm. "Hey, vile monster! I shall set these noble Squirazzis free." He beamed at the cameras. "Free to take my picture for their celebrity photo spreads, that is!"

Lance lunged forward, striking blow after blow at Burnzie. "Action!" he cried out, naming each pose as he grinned for the cameras. "Glamour! Boy next door!" He raised his lance heroically. "Cover shot!"

After a short fight, Burnzie ran away defeated. Lance spun around, eager to smile and pose for the adoring Squirazzi cameras. But the strangest thing happened: None of them seemed the least bit interested in Lance.

In fact, rather than thanking him, one of the camera guys shouted at Lance. "Hey! You chased off Burnzie, the biggest celebrity in Knighton!"

"*What?*" Lance said, gaping at the Squirazzi. "He's a monster! And I just rescued you! And I'm a *celebrity*!"

"Uh-oh," the camera guy said, rolling his eyes at the other Squirazzi. "Poser alert.

Maybe we can still catch Burnzie!" He and the others began to run after the monster.

Lance chased after them. "Hold on! Perhaps you missed this look—I call it . . . *Superstar*!" The forest around him seemed to glow as Lance gave them his most spectacular pose. But no one paid him any attention. Lance was growing desperate and terrified. What if he was—*gulp!*—not popular anymore? How could the cameras prefer ugly old Burnzie to *Lance Richmond*? "Hey, come back! I'll give you some shots from my good side!"

On the other side of the forest, Macy trudged through the dense woods. Suddenly, she, too, was hit by Whiparella's whip. Her eyes turned purple as the magic from The Book of Fear seeped into her body. "Hey!" She raised her mace, ready to fight back. Through

the trees, the only thing she could see was a huge, glowing red monster. Macy recognized the monster right away. It was Sparkks! The knights had defeated Sparkks many times, and Macy knew she could take the ugly, one-eyed beast down easily. This would be a great chance to show the other knights that she really had what it took to be a hero! "Don't move, monster."

"Or what?" Sparkks hissed. "Gonna hit me with your little flowers? Ooh! Maybe you'll blind me with your shiny dress."

"What?" Macy blurted out. She glanced quickly at her weapon, gasping when she noticed it had turned into a bouquet of flowers! She reached up to touch her helmet, then realized it was no longer on her head. "Hey! Where's my mace? And my NEXO KNIGHTS helmet?"

"A knight?" Sparkks scoffed. "Oh, please. You're no *knight*! You're just some pretty little princess out picking flowers."

Macy lunged for the monster. "Why you— ughh!" She stumbled. Looking down, she could see that her armor had become a *princess dress*! "A sparkly dress? Gah!" Macy swatted at the pale-blue dress covered in foofy bows and ribbons. What a nightmare! A fussy dress, no helmet, and a bouquet of stinky flowers? What kind of knight carried flowers? Taking another step, Macy stumbled on the hem of her dress and fell to the ground.

"Aw," Sparkks teased. "Did the pretty little princess fall down?"

Very near the place where Macy was trying to battle Sparkks, Clay was still chasing after

the damsel in distress. "Gotcha!" he said, lunging toward the woman's captor. But instead of getting a hold on her, he landed empty-handed, flat on his face.

"What is with you?" The damsel shouted at him. "I thought you were a brave and noble knight!" She used a silly voice to copy Clay's earlier words. "*'For justice! For honor!'*" Muttering, she added, "More like . . . for *nothing!*"

Clay grumbled under his breath. He ran toward the woman's captor one more time— but again, he missed both the monster and the damsel in distress completely. "This can't be happening!" he wheezed, falling to the ground.

Just then, Macy stumbled toward him. She tripped on her dress and cried out, "Ahhh!"

"Whoa . . . Macy?" Clay said, gaping at her. "What happened to you?"

Macy looked down at her gown. "Is it that bad?"

"Well, uh, no. I've just never seen you look so . . ." Clay trailed off.

"Pathetic?" Macy prompted.

"Elegant," Clay said.

"Now you're just mocking me," Macy frowned. She grunted and tore at the dress, trying to pry away the annoying costume.

Clay shook his head. "No! I mean, at least you haven't completely failed as a knight. Like me. I can't . . ." He drew in a ragged breath. "I can't even rescue a damsel in distress!"

"Let me help," Macy offered. "I'm as tough and fearless as ever!" She tried to charge forward, but her dress was wrapped too

tightly around her legs and she tripped again. Kicking at the fabric, Macy howled, "Stupid dress!"

Things were bad for all of the knights. Lost in the woods, each of them was being tortured by Whiparella's cruel magic. She had poisoned four of them with their own worst nightmares—only Aaron had yet to be hit.

Axl stumbled through the forest, desperate to find food. "Finally!" he said when he came upon another heaping banquet table in a clearing. "Lunch!"

The enormous knight raced forward, nearly crashing into Lance. Lance was still chasing after the band of Squirazzi, who were obviously eager to get away from him.

"C'mon!" Lance pleaded with the photographers. "Just one picture! I'm Lance Richmond! Everyone loves me!"

"Sorry," one of the camera guys said, spinning around. "Never heard of you."

Lance stomped, throwing a teensy tantrum. "You are *so* fired when my dad reaches out to your boss!" Lance raced after the cameras again, barely even noticing Axl as he rushed past.

Axl wasn't bothered, though. He only had eyes for one thing: food! Lots of food. He had never been so hungry, and all he wanted was a tiny bite. He charged toward the tables full of treats, howling when Globlins—once again—beat him to it. They dove on top of a pie, munched on a turkey leg, and ate every last scrap of food before Axl could get any! "What? My food!" Unable to stand the torture any longer, Axl began to weep. Big, horrible sobs that rocked the forest around him. He gazed at the table full of munched-on apple cores and empty

platters and cried for the food he could still smell.

Suddenly, the Squirazzi rushed into the clearing and snapped pictures of him weeping beside the table.

"Really?" Lance shrieked. "Empty plates rate pictures?!"

"Empty plates!" Axl sobbed.

Macy, Clay, Axl, and Lance were all utterly miserable. But farther off in the forest, Aaron was still happy and whistling. Little did he know, he was about to come face-to-face with Whiparella!

The glowing monster leaped out of the forest and snapped her whip at Aaron. But he spun around so quickly that he was able to grab her whip in his bare hand. "Hey!" he barked, narrowing his eyes at her. "What gives?"

Whiparella looked at him, shocked. No one had ever caught her before. It was time to come up with a Plan B. "Oh, uh . . . *this* is what gives!" Whiparella screamed as she began to grow. While Aaron watched from the forest floor, Whiparella grew bigger and bigger, until she was towering over him. "And now," she growled. "I will fill you with fear!"

A giant Whiparella loomed over Aaron, cracking her whips. "Does my huge, frightening self scare you, tiny knight?"

Aaron's eyes grew wide as he took in the sight of the enormous glowing beast. "Whoaaaaa," he marveled. "That is *sick*! Do it again. Do it again!"

"What?" Whiparella gasped. "You're not frightened?"

Aaron shook his head. "No way! That looks awesome!"

"Well, then," Whiparella said, considering her next move. "Perhaps you have a fear of heights!" She lashed her whip at the ground and wrapped it around Aaron's body. She lifted him up, up, up—above the treetops, into the clouds.

When he was high in the sky, Aaron hooted and howled. "Woo-hoooooo!" he cheered. Aaron *loved* the thrill of heights. He slipped out of Whiparella's whip-hold and hopped onto his hover shield. Tilting his board, he rode down Whiparella's enormous side, using her glowing body as a giant, monstrous skate park. "Whoa!" Aaron said when he hopped off at the bottom. "Mad props for the ride, Mullet Mary."

Whiparella shrunk back down to her usual size and glared at Aaron. "What did you say?" She patted her hair, feeling self-conscious.

"This is not a mullet! It's a Dread Lock! And let's see how brave you are now . . . around my creepy crawlies!" She waved her hand in the air, and several Globlins rushed toward Aaron. They sprouted spider legs and skittered around his body, hissing at him.

"I am so totally . . ." Aaron said, eyeing the Globlins warily, ". . . buggin' out!" He hopped on his hover shield again, zooming around the spider-Globlins. As he wound through the pack of critters, the Globlins' legs got all tangled up and they fell into a messy heap. The critters whimpered, helpless, while Aaron whooped with joy. "That is so *off da shield*, yo. What else ya got, Chili Pepper Pam?"

"What?" Whiparella yelled. "That is not my name, either!"

Aaron shrugged. "Whatevs, Hot Links Heidi."

Whiparella growled, her anger mounting with each new name Aaron came up with. People did *not* tease Whiparella! "I am Whiparella!" she howled, flicking her whips in the air. She bared her pointed, fang-like teeth at Aaron, fuming. "With one snap from my whip, I can find your deepest, darkest fear and bring it to life!"

Aaron chuckled. "No way, Whippenstein."

"Yes way!" Whiparella argued. "And it's *Whiparella*! I've crushed all your knight friends. Not with weapons. But with their own worst nightmares." She cackled as she thought about how she'd tortured Axl with delicious food that he couldn't have. "I preyed upon Axl's fear of hunger—the greatest meal, always just out of reach."

Whiparella went on. "Fear of obscurity," she raised her arms in the air, thinking of

Lance and how he had pleaded with the Squirazzi to take just one picture of him. "Lance is a spoiled boy in a world that doesn't even care he exists."

She laughed, thinking about how Macy had struggled to move in her futzy princess dress. "I played with Macy's fear of being a princess who shall *never* become a true knight."

And then there was Clay, who was so desperate to prove himself to be a hero. Whiparella cackled. "Clay is overcome by his fear of failing. Not just the damsel in distress I created, but he fears failing with your beloved Knights' Code as well."

Aaron nodded, as though he understood. He leaned back against a giant boulder, sucking down a soda. "Good times. Right, *Wimp-arella*?"

"Stop that!" Whiparella screeched. Her

yellow eyes glowed with fury. "And tell me why my fear magic has no effect on you? I've got no sense of any fear from you!"

"That's because I've got NO FEAR!" Aaron roared. He lifted his bow and strummed on it like it was a guitar, screaming out a rock beat. "None whatsoever. Woo-hoo!" He raised his arms and pumped his fists in the air.

"But that can't be," Whiparella hissed. "Everyone has fears. Some are just less obvious. How about these classics..." She whistled, summoning up more scary things. First, she conjured up a monster standing at a chalkboard. On Whiparella's cue, the creature raked its long, talon-like fingernails across the board. A horrible screeching noise echoed through the forest. Whiparella covered her ears—the sound was horrible!

But Aaron loved it. "Ooh! Lemme play some harmony!" He pulled out his bow-guitar and jammed along with the music of the nails on the chalkboard.

Whiparella frowned. Then she got another idea. "Paging Doctor Sparkks, DDS." She grinned. "Everyone fears the dentist!" She shoved Aaron into a huge dentist chair, cackling as the dentist hovered over him with a whizzing dental drill.

"Woo!" Aaron cheered from inside his seat. "Nothin' to fear. I got *no* cavities. I'm a big brusher, yo. 'Cause plaque is whack!" He opened his mouth wide, letting the dentist have at him.

Whiparella was growing more and more frustrated with each failed attempt. "*Hmm.* Ha! The naked truth! That never fails to destroy you!" With a quick flip of her hand,

Whiparella zapped the clothes and armor right off Aaron's body.

Holding his shield in front of himself, Aaron glanced around the forest nervously. "Whoa, where did my armor go?"

Whiparella laughed. "You're completely exposed for all the world to see. Nowhere to hide now. Within moments you'll be—"

Aaron strutted proudly through the clearing. He announced, "I'm rockin' the commando look!"

"What?!" Whiparella growled.

"I've never felt so free!" Aaron told her. "Thanks, Whipper-Snapper."

Whiparella howled. She was *furious*! And she was also out of ideas. Furious, she stormed off to plot her revenge.

Aaron had stopped Whiparella from cap-turing him, but he still needed help to save his

friends. *If only there was a NEXO Power that could make the other knights, um, unafraid . . .*

As if in answer to Aaron's thoughts, he heard Merlok 2.0's voice through his shield. "Prepare for NEXO Scan!"

This was exactly what Aaron needed! He raised his shield in excitement. "NEXOOOOO Knight!" he called.

"NEXO Power: Lion of Bravery!" Merlok 2.0 announced.

A moment later, Aaron's shield surged with new power as the NEXO Power downloaded. Aaron lifted his shield, sending beams of white, magical light out into the dark forest. Then he raced through the woods. It was time to save his friends from their worst nightmares!

Nearby, Clay had grown weak with the effort of trying to rescue the damsel in distress. He crawled through the forest, trying to catch the woman and her captor. Macy followed close behind.

"Please, monster," he begged, gasping for breath. The monster raced in circles around him, the woman clutching the monsters shoulders so she wouldn't fall off. Clay reached out to them, begging, "Stop . . . I must save the damsel. Or else . . . my honor, my chivalry . . . all that matters." His voice broke. "I have failed."

Aaron burst out of the woods at that moment. Waving his shield proudly, he cried, "You talkin' about *this* damsel?" He shot two arrows—one at the monster, and one at the damsel in distress. The monster dissolved the moment the arrow struck.

While Clay watched, horrified, the woman hissed . . . and then she, too, morphed into a monster! She had been a creature disguised by Whiparella's powers all along. Aaron shot another arrow at the creature, then whooped when it dissolved. "Boo-ya!"

"Aaron?" Clay said, looking from the two monsters to his fellow knight. "What are you doing here?" His eyes bulged out of his head, then he looked down, embarrassed. "And where's your armor?"

Aaron glanced down at his still-naked body. With a casual shrug, he explained, "Ah,

some whip lady took 'em. I think she was trying to scare me."

"Well, uh," Clay cringed. "Honestly, your lack of modesty is scaring me a bit."

Aaron grinned. "Oh . . . sorry. Be right back." He dashed through the woods, returning a moment later wearing a full set of green-and-gray armor.

"Aaron," Clay asked. "Tell us more about this 'whip lady'?"

"Oh," Aaron said. "Well, she snaps you with her whip and your worst fears come to life."

"What?" Macy asked. Everything that had happened in the woods was suddenly starting to make more sense.

Aaron proudly added, "But I have no fear! Woo-hoo! So it was just kinda fun for me."

"We must find the others," Clay told Aaron and Macy. "But . . . the fear."

Aaron shook his head. "Hey, no sweat, bro. You still probably got her scary magic in ya. No worries. I'll take the lead."

Clay nodded gratefully, then he and Macy followed Aaron deeper into the forest. By the time they reached Axl, the huge knight was completely exhausted—and starving.

"So hungry," he moaned. He grabbed for another drumstick on the table. But a Globlin got hold of it at the same time and the creature and Axl played tug-of-war with the chunk of meat. "Please," Axl begged, his body collapsing from hunger. "One bite . . ."

Suddenly, one of Aaron's arrows zipped into the clearing. When it struck the drumstick, the meat dissolved into nothing. Aaron soared into the clearing on his hover shield and batted at the Globlins with his bow. The

little monsters scattered. One by one, Aaron hit each of them with arrows and the creatures turned into dust.

Now, the only one left to save was Lance. As Aaron, Axl, Macy, and Clay came upon their famous friend in the forest, they could hear him begging. "C'mon," Lance pleaded with the Squirazzi. "Please! I'm Knighton's most celebrated celebutante."

"What'd you say your name was?" one of the photographers asked.

"Lance! Lance Richmond!"

"Oh," the Squirazzi said. "Yeah, never heard of you."

Before Lance could respond, Axl came crashing through the trees. Aaron released one of his arrows, and the first Squirazzi disappeared in a *poof*! One by one, the rest followed. Lance grabbed one of their cameras and took pictures as his fellow knights

bashed the magical monsters. The camera flashed just as one of the Globlins was conked over the head. Lance cheered, "Now *that's* what I call a 'cover shot!'"

While the knights celebrated their victory, Whiparella returned to Jestro and The Book of Monsters to await further instructions. She told Jestro about her encounter with Aaron, feeling embarrassed that she had failed. She hung her head as she told him how she had failed—all thanks to Aaron.

"What do you mean he had 'no fear?'" Jestro wailed.

"Every one of them crumbled before the terror of their own worst nightmares," Whiparella told him. She lowered her voice to add, "Except the archer. My magic didn't work. He was afraid of *nothing*."

Jestro spun around and screamed at The Book of Monsters. "Are you kidding me? I thought you said she could scare anyone?"

The Book of Monsters asked, "Did you try the creepy crawlers?"

Whiparella nodded.

"What about the dentist?" The Book of Monsters said.

Whiparella nodded again. Sulking, she said, "I even gave him an 'out-of-clothes experience.'"

The monsters gathered around in the forest all gasped. Sparkks asked, "Completely naked? In public?!"

"Yikes!" Sparkks yowled. "Talk about nightmares!"

The Book of Monsters grumbled, "Wow. I hate the dentist. But that didn't even faze him, huh?"

"No," Whiparella whined. "He called me all kinds of names, like 'Hot Links Heidi' and . . ." She sniffed. "'Wimp-arella.'"

The other monsters all gasped again. "Aww," Sparkks said sadly, patting her on the shoulder. "That's terrible."

The Scurrier who had spent the whole night torturing Clay chimed in, "It doesn't even make any sense!"

Burnzie shook his head. "You poor thing. Do you need a hug?"

Whiparella nodded gratefully, and all her monster pals squeezed her into a friendly hug.

The Book of Monsters whispered, "'Wimp-arella'? That's pretty good."

Jestro growled at the book and the creatures. "Stop that! All of you, stop that! There will be none of that while I'm here! *No*

58

hugging until we stop those knights! That Aaron must have *something* he's scared of."

"Yeah," came a voice from the woods. It was Aaron! He added, "I'm scared of your terrible comedy routines, Jestro."

Jestro turned just in time to see the knights marching toward him, ready for battle. Jestro shouted, "Now's your chance, Whiparella! Hit him with everything you've got!"

Whiparella looked up from the hug. Her eyes narrowed. She flicked her whips. Then she hissed, "Yes! I don't believe *anyone* fears nothing!" Her whips glowed with magic as she swung both of them at Aaron. She put all her strength into the attack.

But Aaron was ready. He fired back with two arrows. Each one hit one of her whips, sending them backward—straight toward Jestro!

With a *smack*, they hit the evil court jester right in the face. Jestro frowned as the whips' magic sunk in. His eyes glowed. He wobbled and tried to focus on the forest around him. "Uh..." he asked, woozy. "Was that supposed to happen?"

"Whoa," The Book of Monsters gasped, cringing. "You were hit with double snaps! Things might get a little scary."

Jestro swayed as the magic took hold. He blinked, and when his droopy eyes opened again, he was back in the Joustdome at the castle. He was on stage, performing for everyone. "Wait," he mumbled aloud. He wasn't sure if he was in the forest or the castle. It was the most real dream he'd ever had! "Where am I?"

The Book of Monsters told him, "Don't worry: you're just in the middle of a very severe fear-dream."

Jestro could hear The Book of Monsters speaking to him, but the voice sounded far away. He looked around the Joustdome, staring nervously up into the stands filled with jeering crowds. He muttered, "But . . . but, I'm in the Joustdome. The last time I looked like a fool. And there are knights here, too. Aaron . . ." He blinked and swayed. "Oh, I get it! Aaron said the only thing he feared was my terrible comedy routine. So now . . . I shall destroy him!" He stood up and lunged for Aaron. But suddenly, the only thing he could see was people—laughing at him. Everyone was making fun of him!

"Uh," The Book of Monsters told him. "Aaron was only joking about that before. This is actually *your* worst nightmare."

"It is?" Jestro whispered. He glanced around again. All he could see was a sea of faces, and they were all laughing at him.

In the dream, people were screaming, "This guy's awful!" and "He's the worst jester ever!"

Jestro covered his head. "No! This can't be happening. Not again . . . keep it together!" Suddenly, he was holding a sword, a mace, a halberd, and some arrows. While everyone watched, Jestro tried to juggle them—but they all just rained down around him. He spun plates on sticks, but they all crashed and broke on the Joustdome floor. "Nooooo!" Jestro moaned, then dropped to the ground. He closed his eyes, hoping to hide from the scene inside the nightmare.

The evil jester curled into a ball on the forest floor, his body twitching with fear. All of his monsters leaned over him, waiting for him to wake up from his nightmare.

"Uh . . ." Macy said, staring at Jestro wide-eyed. "Is he okay?"

The Book of Monsters gazed down at its master—then looked at the knights. "Yeah," the book said. "But now it's *my* worst fear. We've lost again." The Book of Monsters screamed at the other creatures. "Grab him! And let's scram!" Sparkks and Burnzie snatched Jestro off the forest floor. Then the book, all the monsters, and Jestro fled in fear.

CHAPTER 6

By the next morning, everything had gone back to normal in the village of Spittoon. Now that The Book of Fear was gone, the knights were quickly able to restore order to the tough town. People were spitting and snarling at each other, just like the good old days. "Watch your step!" one guy screamed.

"Have a terrible day," yelled another.

When the Fortrex rolled out of town, the villagers waved their fists and spit and pushed one another around some more. It

was life as usual in Spittoon—and the knights were off on their next adventure.

"I still think we should have chased after them and . . . *wham!*" Aaron said, slamming his fist into the palm of his hand. He couldn't believe they had let Jestro and The Book of Monsters get away without a fight!

Clay shook his head. "The Knights' Code says we're supposed to defend the down-trodden. Jestro seemed pretty down." He thought back to the previous night, cringing at the memory of his failed rescue. Even though it had all been a dream, it had been a *terrible* dream, and Clay couldn't stop thinking about how he had failed to save the damsel in distress. "But then, I utterly failed the whole 'Knights' Code' thing, didn't I?"

Macy patted him on the shoulder. "Aw, c'mon. Don't be so hard on yourself, Clay. We all fell for that slithery monster's tricks."

"Not Aaron," Clay said. "The Fear Monster looked for his deepest fear and all she found was *nothing*."

Merlok 2.0 cut in, "Ah, but sometimes 'nothing' is the greatest fear of all."

Clay looked stumped. "Sorry, Merlok 2.0, but that makes no sense. Aaron is the truest of knights."

"I suggest you read your *Knights' Code* again, Clay," said Merlok 2.0. "It says: 'We are many, we are one.'"

Macy nodded. "Yeah, and that means we're a team. We've each got our own strengths that make the team stronger. And it makes each of us stronger, too."

Clay considered this for a moment. He wasn't so sure he agreed.

But Macy went on, "The truest of knights—like *you*, Clay—should understand that."

Clay sighed. Sure, working as a team was important. But he also worried that he wasn't as tough as he ought to be. He was on a quest to be the best. "Yes, Macy," he said. "But I don't know. I still wish I was like Aaron—afraid of nothing!"

Merlok 2.0 raised his eyebrow. He stroked his beard. Suddenly, he had an idea. It was time to show the knights that *everyone* had a fear—you just had to find it. A moment later, the wizard's computerized hologram faded away. Then the castle slammed to a stop and all the power went out. Aaron crashed to the ground when even his hover shield powered down.

"Hey," Aaron said from the floor. "What gives?"

Ava punched at buttons on the computer, trying to power everything back up. "Sorry," Ava said, shrugging. "Some kind of power surge. Merlok 2.0 is offline."

"Is he okay?" Clay asked, concerned.

"He's fine," Robin told the more experienced knights. "But we'll have to shut down everything in the castle to get him back up and running again."

"Even my shield?" Aaron said, a note of panic creeping into his voice.

"No choice," Robin shrugged. "We've gotta make sure there's no electrical interference while we reboot."

"Yeah," Ava agreed. "The system is very fragile. So stay completely silent and still during the reboot. Do *nothing*!"

"What?" Aaron shrieked. His body began to tremble. In a whisper, he asked, "But,

but . . . how am I supposed to stay still? How long will this take?"

Quietly, Robin told him, "According to this message from Merlok, it will take about ten minutes."

"I have to do *nothing*?!" Aaron screamed. "For a whole *ten minutes*?!" His eyes went wide, and he began to sweat. His body was shaking and trembling.

Lance cocked an eyebrow. "Everything okay, Aaron?"

Aaron shuddered. He was so overcome by the idea of doing nothing that he wasn't even able to speak. "Uhh," he moaned. His body began to twitch and his face was filled with terror. "Ugh . . . not moving. I can't take *nothing*! Ahhhhh!" He threw his arms up in the air and screamed. He ran from the room and the other knights were left to stare after him.

A moment later, the system roared to life again. The hologram of Merlok reappeared— and the wizard was smirking.

"What was *that* all about?" Clay asked.

"Oh," Merlok said, chuckling. "You just saw Aaron's greatest fear: when there is nothing to do. As The Fear Monster said, he is literally afraid of . . . *nothing*!"

"Really?" Macy said. It seemed so silly— and impossible.

"No one is completely fearless, Clay," Merlok said. "Not even the truest of knights."

Clay nodded, finally understanding. He grinned at their trusty wizard advisor. "Merlok . . . you didn't have anything to do with that system reboot, did you?"

The orange hologram of a wizard shrugged. "What? Me?" The corners of his mustache lifted in a smile. "Uh, no . . . I'm a wizard. Not a rebooting, techno-mathingy

guy who just happened to bump into a few switches here and there that go beep beep boop."

Macy's mouth hung open. She lifted one eyebrow and whispered to Clay, "What is he talking about?"

Merlok 2.0 continued to make beeping sounds while the rest of the knights shook their heads, confused.

"I don't know," Clay said. "I'm afraid to ask. Very afraid."

Macy nodded and laughed. "We all are sometimes, aren't we?"

Macy and Clay exchanged a smile. Merlok 2.0 continued to *beep* and *boop*, while Axl settled in at a table to eat until he was stuffed. Lance brushed his hair and smiled at himself in the mirror. And Aaron hopped onto his hover shield and raced around the castle, relieved that he hadn't been forced to spend

ten minutes doing nothing. The thought was far too terrifying!

As the Fortrex rolled on toward the knights' next adventure, it seemed that things were back to normal—for now. But even as they all relaxed into their favorite activities, the NEXO KNIGHTS team had no doubt their next quest would find them soon. And they would be ready. Separated and alone, the knights had given into their fears. But as a team they were strong enough to overcome any scary challenge. Together, they would restore harmony to the Realm and defeat Jestro and his monsters once and for all!